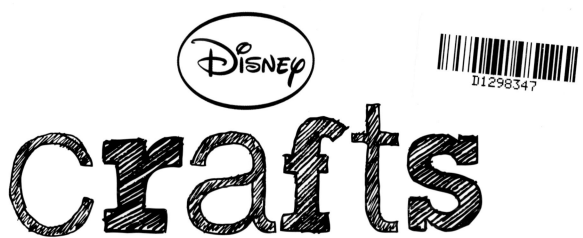

crafts

Over 30 Minnie project ideas to make and create.

Bath · New York · Cologne · Melbourne · Delhi
Hong Kong · Shenzhen · Singapore · Amsterdam

Written by DropCap Ltd.
Edited by DropCap Ltd. and Gillian Kirschner
Designed by Karl Tall and Vanessa Mee
Photography by Darren Sawyer
Step-by-step illustrations by Philip McIvor
Crafts by Susan Hunter-Jones and Katy Rhodes
Paper engineering by Bag of Badgers
Production by Charlene Vaughan
Photograph models: Heather Partridge and Charlene Vaughan

This edition published by Parragon Books Ltd in 2014 and distributed by

Parragon Inc.
440 Park Avenue South, 13th Floor
New York, NY 10016
www.parragon.com

ISBN 978-1-4723-3427-5

Printed in China

Tips for Parents and Guardians

This book is for parents and children to come together and be creative! Making crafts with young children can be so much fun and will give them (and you!) a sense of achievement.

Developing children's skills

Every project in this book includes at least one task that a young child can do themselves, with relative ease. What seems like a simple task to you—applying glue to a piece of paper, painting a badge, or arranging some buttons on a collage—is not so easy for a small child, and doing them can instill a sense of pride.

Children go through several developmental stages with regard to arts and crafts—from scribbles (about age 2), to assigning meaning to shapes drawn (about age 5), and the creation of three-dimensional objects (about age 8). Although the pace at which each child progresses may differ, important skills can be developed through doing craft activities. These include:

- Learning skills
- Logic, problem solving
- Basic math skills (measuring)
- Reading (looking at directions or reading a recipe)
- Following sequential directions
- Creative and artistic sensibility
- Self-esteem and a sense of uniqueness
- Fine and gross motor skills
- Hand-eye coordination
- Cleaning skills (including responsibility)
- Understanding that creating things is fun!

How to use this book

The crafts included in this book all require adult supervision (and usually hands-on help), especially with a child under 5. However, for each craft, there are steps your child can do, either on their own or with your help.

When you see this symbol  **it means that you will need to help your child or just watch over them and offer guidance.**

The first step is to pick a craft appropriate to your child's ability and then read through the instructions from beginning to end. That way, you will know what materials and tools you will need.

Next, if your child is able, encourage them to read familiar numbers and words out loud. You can also discuss concepts such as "one half" by showing that if you cut one whole cardboard tube into two equal parts, you have two halves.

Finally, although directions for these crafts are often very specific in order to ensure clarity, remember that part of the fun of making crafts is to be creative. Experiment with colors, patterns, and recycled objects. There's no wrong way to do something when you are creating! Don't worry if the end result doesn't look exactly like the photo—half the fun of crafting is developing your own style and expression.

Recycling

Save things from around the house that can be used for crafting:

- Cardboard (sheets and rolls)
- Colored construction paper
- Kitchen sponges
- Paper plates, bowls, cups
- String
- Ribbon
- Yarn
- Newspapers and magazines
- Cotton and cotton swabs
- Gift wrap
- Fabric
- Tissue paper
- Craft sticks
- Wooden spoons

Craft tools

With these tools in your art and craft kit you'll always be ready to create a masterpiece:

- Scissors
- Craft glue
- Glue stick
- Ruler
- Pencil
- Marker pens
- Coloring pencils
- Clear tape
- Double-sided tape
- Masking tape
- Paintbrushes
- Craft paints
- Fabric paints

Handy extras

You might already have some of these at home, but if not you can find them in craft stores. It's useful to have them ready and waiting for when you're feeling crafty!

- Buttons
- Sequins
- Felt
- Glitter or glitter glue
- Beads

Useful templates

Tracing from templates is a useful method of copying shapes that will be transferred onto card stock or fabric and then cut out. Some of the projects in this book use templates, others require you and your child to draw easy shapes freehand onto card stock.

For symmetrical shapes, such as a heart, fold the card stock in half. Draw half the shape against the fold and cut the shape out. When you unfold, your template will be perfectly neat and symmetrical. Don't throw your templates away—keep them in your craft kit in case you want to use them again!

Templates

To copy one of the templates from inside this book (pages 44–47), use a sheet of tracing paper (or greaseproof paper from the kitchen). Help your child trace over the template with a pencil. Turn the paper over, retrace the template onto card stock, and then cut out the shape.

For a character, help your child trace over the template with a pencil. Turn the paper over and retrace the template. Then, flip the paper over again so the character is the right way round. Tip: make sure it matches the template in the back of the book! Place your tracing onto a piece of card stock, and go back over the template. Take the paper away to reveal your template copy, ready for you to cut out and use.

Sewing skills

Sometimes it might be quicker to glue things together, but sewing can make your projects stronger, neater, and more stylish. Teaching your child to sew also helps to develop their hand-eye coordination.

Buttons

To sew on a button, thread your needle and tie a knot at the end of the thread. Hold the button in place and push the needle up through the fabric and one of the button holes. Take the needle back down through the opposite hole and the fabric underneath. Repeat until the button feels secure, then tie a knot at the end of the thread. Trim the thread close to the knot, but not so close that it's easily undone.

Running stitch

1. Thread your needle and tie a knot at the end of the thread. Bring the needle up through the fabric. Pull firmly so the knot is against the back of the fabric.
2. Push the needle back down about one-quarter inch along your fabric. Pull the thread all the way through. That's your first stitch!
3. Keep going, moving the needle in and out of the fabric to make more stitches about one-quarter inch apart. Tie a knot under the fabric at the end when you're done, or go back over your last stitch a few times. Trim the thread close to the knot, but not so close that it's easily undone.

How to make papier-mâché

There are a few crafts in this book that are made from papier-mâché. There are different ways to make papier-mâché, but this is the easiest.

You will need:
- Newspapers (torn into strips or squares)
- Bowl
- Craft glue and brush
- Water

1. Mix 2 parts craft glue with 1 part water in a bowl. The specific craft will instruct you what to mold your papier-mâché around (e.g. a balloon or a bowl). To help the papier-mâché slide off more easily when it is dry, cover the mold object in petroleum jelly.
2. Using a brush, paint the strips of newspaper with the craft glue mixture. Lay the pieces of newspaper one at a time over the object, then brush more glue over the top. When you've finished the first layer, leave to dry. Then, cover with two more layers and leave them to dry. It may take a day or two to dry completely.

Star ratings

Each craft has a star rating. This will help you decide which craft you have time to create and which one is most suitable for your child to do themselves.

 ★★★

This is a simple craft that your child will need little hands-on help to create. These crafts should take the least time between making and playing!

 ★★★

Your child will probably need some help, but there will be steps that your child can do for themselves. It will take some time to create and may require time for parts of the craft to dry.

 ★★★

This is a more challenging craft and may include more developed crafting skills, such as sewing. There are parts that a child can do on their own or perhaps with a little help. These crafts include time to prepare or dry.

Minnie's happy hats

With this party hat, complete with adorable ears and pretty bow, you'll want to have a Minnie party every day!

You will need:

- Paper dinner plate
- Card stock (8.5in x 11in, black)
- Pencil (white)
- Scissors
- Ruler
- Double-sided tape
- Cup
- Ribbon (black, 0.25in x 20in)
- Templates on page 45
- Posterboard (red polka dot)
- Small square of thick cardboard

1 Ask your child to place the paper plate on the sheet of black card so that about three-quarters of it sits on the card. Draw around the plate with a white pencil.

2 Use a ruler to draw a line across the widest part of the circle, then put a dot at the halfway mark. Draw another line out from the center point so you have a shape a little bigger than a semicircle. Cut it out.

3 Put a strip of double-sided tape along one straight edge. Peel off the tape and make the shape into a cone. Press along the taped edge to secure the shape.

4 For the ears, put a cup onto the black card and draw around it. Use the ruler to draw a tab shape next to the circle. Repeat to make two ear shapes with tabs.

5 Cut out the two ear shapes and fold the tabs over. Put double-sided tape on each tab and stick the ears to the top of the cone, with the tabs facing backward. Cut the ribbon in half and stick each piece on the inside of the hat with double-sided tape.

6 👥 Trace the bow and oval templates and transfer onto red polka-dot posterboard. Cut them out. Tape a small piece of cardboard to the back of the oval shape, then stick it on the middle of the bow for a 3D effect. Tape the bow shape to the front of the hat.

Make different hats in your favorite colors to match all your outfits! Decorate them with your Minnie stickers and a ribbon tied into a bow.

Make hats for your friends so you can all be members of the Minnie fan club!

Minnie's bow-tastic shoes

Who says sneakers aren't pretty? With polka-dot shoelaces and a cool tag, you can wear this fancy footwear anywhere!

You will need:

- Scissors
- Ribbon (red polka dot, 0.5in x 80in)
- Pair of sneakers
- Pencil (white)
- Template on page 45
- Posterboard (black)
- Hole punch
- Ribbon (red, 0.5in x 10in)
- Double-sided tape
- Ribbon (black, 0.25in x 10in)
- Ribbon (red polka dot, 0.75in x 20in)
- Extra-strong double-sided tape

1 Cut the 80-inch red polka-dot ribbon in half. Use one piece to thread down through the top left eyelet of your shoe. Pull about 30-inches through, then thread the end up through the bottom right eyelet.

2 Now thread the ribbon down through the bottom left eyelet, so the ribbon lies flat. Continue in the same way until the shoe is laced, then tie the ribbon in a pretty bow. Lace the second shoe in the same way with the other half of the ribbon.

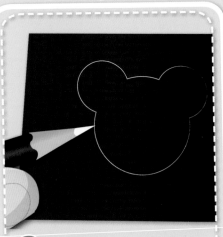

3 To make the tag, ask your child to use a white pencil to draw around the template of Minnie's head on page 45 on to black posterboard.

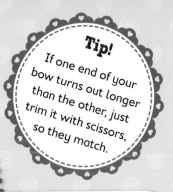

Tip!
If one end of your bow turns out longer than the other, just trim it with scissors, so they match.

④ 👥 Cut out the shape and use the hole punch to make a hole in one ear. Tie a small bow in the red ribbon.

⑤ Tape the red bow onto the head, then thread the thin black ribbon through the hole and attach the tag to the shoe through an eyelet.

⑥ Tie the thick red polka-dot ribbon in a bow and use extra-strong double-sided tape to attach it to the front of one of the shoes.

These sneakers are perfect for when Minnie needs to combine comfort with style!

9

Buttons 'n' beads jewelry

It's so quick and easy to create your own must-have Minnie-inspired matching set of jewelry!

You will need:

★ ☆ ☆

Necklace:
- Ribbon (red, 0.25in x 24in)
- Blunt embroidery needle
- Selection of buttons and beads (red and white)
- Two small, four-hole buttons
- Scissors

Ring:
- Ribbon (red, 0.25in x 10in)
- Button (white)
- Smaller button (red)

1  For the necklace, thread the red ribbon onto a blunt embroidery needle.

Minnie loves to shop, but she enjoys designing her own jewelry even more!

2 Ask your child to choose some beads and buttons. Thread the needle through the first button, then slide it to the middle of the ribbon.

3 Thread about 10 more buttons and beads onto the ribbon. Use a four-hole button last and sew through it twice to hold everything in place.

4 Thread the needle through the other end of the ribbon and add buttons and beads, ending with a four-hole button as before. Remove the needle, trim the ends of the ribbon, and tie loosely into a bow.

Experiment with different colored ribbon, buttons, and beads to create a line of new and fantastic jewelry for your friends!

1 For the ring, thread the ribbon through the needle. Push up through one hole of a white button and slide it to the middle. Now thread up through a smaller red button and back down through the other hole, then through the white button again.

2 Push the buttons together, turn them over, and tie the ribbon around your child's finger in a secure bow. Trim the ends.

Fabulous fashion box

Stylish storage is so this season! Keep all your treasures safe in this practical, pretty box.

Tip!

This is messy work! Before you start, cover your work surfaces with sheets of old newspaper.

You will need:

- Craft glue, brush, and water
- Mixing bowl
- Old newspapers
- Plastic wrap
- Two containers, same size and shape, with parallel sides (e.g. yogurt cups)
- Scissors
- Paper (red)
- Small round stickers (white)
- Paintbrush
- Ribbon (black polka dot)
- Paper cut into thin strips (black)

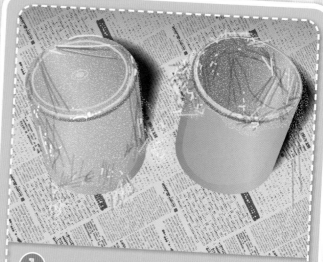

1 Cover the outside of the first container and the inside of the second container with plastic wrap.

2 Following the instructions on page 5, cover the outside of the first container in papier-mâché. Then help your child cover the outside of the first container with a thicker layer of papier-mâché, to the height you want your box to be.

3 Cover the inside of the second container with papier-mâché to roughly the same height as the first. To make the box extra sturdy, let the papier-mâché dry overnight, then apply another layer or two of newspaper to both containers.

4 Set the papier-mâché in a warm place and let it dry, then gently remove each piece from the containers. Trim the rough edges of the top with scissors. You now have the base and lid of your box!

5 Mix up another batch of glue mixture (see page 5). Have your child tear red paper into small pieces. Next, soak them in the glue mixture and paste them to the papier-mâché boxes, making sure the newspaper is completely covered.

Tip!
If you don't have red paper, cover the dry box in white paper and paint with red acrylic paint.

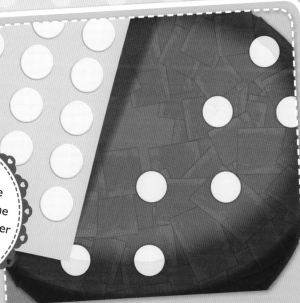

6 When the red paper is completely dry, decorate the slightly bigger box, which will be the lid, with white stickers to make polka dots.

7 Brush a layer of glue mixture over the whole lid and leave to dry. Don't worry if the mixture looks cloudy—the glue will dry clear.

8 Cut two equal lengths of the ribbon. Glue the end of one piece to the inside edge of the lid, then glue the other piece to the opposite side.

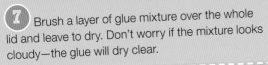

9 Turn the lid over so you can tie the two ribbons in a knot at the center of the lid. Make a loop in the end of each length of ribbon and knot the loops together to make a pretty bow. Trim the ends and dab them with craft glue to prevent them fraying. To finish, glue the strips of black paper to create stripes around the smaller box, which will be the bottom, then cover with a layer of glue mixture and leave to dry.

Cover old boxes in papier-mâché to create fabulous fashion boxes in different colors, shapes, and sizes!

Get the Minnie look!

Add a dash of fashion genius to your hairstyle with a mouse-tastic set of Minnie ears!

You will need:

- Template on page 44
- Pencil (white)
- Posterboard (black)
- Scissors
- Plastic headband (black)
- Craft glue and brush
- Ribbon (red polka dot, 0.75in x 20in)
- Thread (red)

Make a fashion statement with hair accessories. If the bow fits, wear it!

1 Trace the ear template on page 44 and transfer the shape onto black posterboard with a white pencil. Cut it out, then repeat so you have two ears.

2 Help your child position the ears on each side of the top of the headband. Wrap the long tab at the base of each ear around the headband and glue it to the back of the ear with craft glue. Leave to dry.

3 Hold the polka-dot ribbon between your finger and thumb and make a loop on the left. Make a second loop on the right, then repeat, so that you have two loops on each side of your thumb. The ends of the ribbon should be behind your loops.

4 Turn the bow over. Take a short length of red thread and tie it tightly around the middle of the bow, snipping off the loose ends.

5 Glue the bow in position at the top of the headband, between the two Minnie ears.

6 Take a short length of the ribbon, loop it around both the bow and headband, then glue it in place.

Tip!
To stop the ribbon from fraying, run some glue along the cut ends and let them dry.

Shopping in style!

This tote definitely gets Minnie's vote—it's easy to make and super trendy!

You will need:

- Templates on page 45
- Scissors
- Paper
- Old newspapers
- Clear tape
- Plain cloth tote bag
- Fabric paint (red, pink, and white)
- Paintbrush
- Hole punch
- Card stock
- Iron

1 Use the bow template on page 45 and draw it on a sheet of paper. Fold the paper in half and cut out the bow. When you unfold the paper, you'll have a bow-shaped stencil.

2 Now for the messy part! Cover your work surface with old newspapers, then lay the bag flat. Slip a newspaper inside it to stop the paint from seeping through.

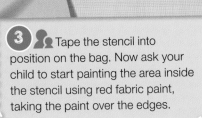

3 Tape the stencil into position on the bag. Now ask your child to start painting the area inside the stencil using red fabric paint, taking the paint over the edges.

Tip!

Before you start your shopping spree, fix the paint by ironing the bag. Make sure to follow the manufacturer's instructions.

4 Carefully lift the stencil off the bag to show a bow shape with crisp, neat edges. Leave to dry.

5 To make the polka dots, use a hole punch to make some holes in a piece of card. Put the card on the bow and ask your child to paint the holes white. Repeat to make polka dots all over the bow.

6 As you did in Step 1, make heart-shaped stencils from the templates. Stencil red and pink hearts in a pretty pattern over the front of the bag.

Got the stencil bug? Take brightly colored tote bags and stencil polka dots or hearts all over them.

Funky pencil pot

With this cute holder, you'll always have pencils on hand when you feel the urge to make a shopping list!

You will need:

- Card stock (red, black, cream, yellow, and white)
- Scissors
- Recycled container (e.g. bread crumb container)
- Double-sided tape
- Craft glue and brush
- Frilly ribbon (red polka dot, 1.25in x 12in)
- Ribbon (red polka dot, 1in x 26in)
- Empty pot (2.25in diameter)
- Templates on page 46
- Felt-tip marker pens (black and pink)
- Two small red bows

1 Wrap the red card around the container, covering the sides. Tape in place and trim the edges, if necessary. Glue a 1.25in strip of black card around the top and another one, 0.75in wide, around the bottom.

2 Put a thin line of craft glue around the pot, slightly lower than the middle. Glue on the frilly ribbon.

3 Cut the longer red ribbon in half and then glue one half above the frilly ribbon.

4 For the ears, ask your child to draw around a cup to make two circles on black card. Cut the ears out and cut up to the middle of each one. Slot the ears on each side of the top of the pot.

5 Using the template, cut Minnie's face out of cream card and her eyes out of white card. Glue the white eye shapes to the face and add details with felt-tip marker pens. Glue the face onto the pot.

6 Tie the leftover red polka-dot ribbon in a bow and glue it between Minnie's ears. Using the templates, make two hands from white card and two shoes from yellow card. Glue the shoes to the bottom of the pot and the hands to the sides. Finally, add little red bows to the shoes.

Time to hit the mall!

With this adorable bag charm, you can take Minnie with you on shopping trips. You never know when you'll need her style advice!

You will need:

- 2 cups all-purpose flour
- 1 cup table salt
- 1 cup water
- Mixing bowl
- Spoon
- Rolling pin
- Template on page 45
- Paper
- Pencil
- Knife
- Paper clip
- Acrylic paint (cream, black, white, and red)
- Paintbrush
- Glitter glue (red and silver)
- Thread
- Beads to decorate

★★☆

1 Help your child mix the flour and salt in the bowl, then gradually stir in the water. The mixture should be stiff, like pastry. If it's too dry, add more water. If it is too sticky, add more flour. Ask your child to knead the dough for about 10 minutes. Take it out of the bowl and let it rest for 10 more minutes.

2 Roll out the dough with the rolling pin until it is about 0.75-inches thick.

3 Trace around the face template on page 45 and cut it out. Place the template on the dough and cut around it with a knife.

4 Turn the shape over and gently push a paper clip into the dough, with the loop just visible at the top of Minnie's head. This will be used to attach a thread for hanging. Leave the dough to dry in a warm place for at least 48 hours.

If you don't have a paper clip, use the end of a paintbrush to create a hole near the top of the head.

5 Paint Minnie's bow, ears, and face then leave them to dry. Ask your child to add red glitter glue to the bow. Add silver glitter glue dots to her bow. Tie thread through the hole or paper clip to make a loop for hanging the charm. Thread beads over the loop and tie in place for the finishing touch!

It's all about Minnie!

Tip!
You can draw your own Minnie or you can use the stickers of her face and bow from your sticker sheet.

Let's dress to impress!

Wow! This limited edition Minnie creation is going to be the cutest skirt of the season!

You will need:

★★★

- Tape measure
- Fabric (red polka dot, 40in x 45in*)
- Scissors
- Pencil
- Ruler
- Pins
- Needle
- Cotton thread (red and black)
- Iron
- Ribbon (black, 0.25in x 60in)
- Elastic (0.4in x 60in)
- Ribbon (black, 1.5in x 40in)

* The dimensions of the fabric will depend on the size and age of the child. Please adjust the dimensions according to the child's size and height. You can measure a skirt to help you.

1 Measure from your child's waist to her knees and add 3.25-inches to allow for the hem. Cut the fabric to this length. Fold the fabric in half across the width, with the pattern on the inside.

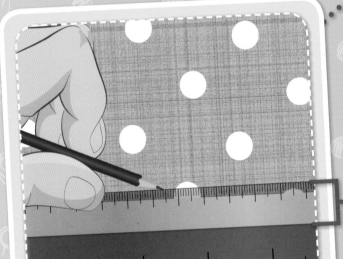

This is the 0.75in

2 Using a ruler and pencil, draw a line 0.75-inches in from the edge of the material. Pin through both layers of fabric to hold it in place.

24

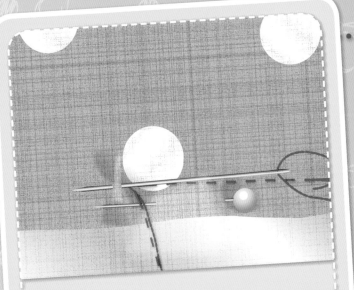

3 👥 Sew running stitch (see page 4) in red thread along the pencil mark. When you have sewn to the end of the line, knot the thread and snip off any loose ends. This will be the back seam of the skirt.

4 👥 Now lay the fabric so the seam is in the middle and press it flat with an iron. Fold a 1.25-inch hem at the bottom and a 2-inch hem at the top of the skirt, then press along the folds with the iron. This will make it easier to sew the hems.

5 👥 Turn your material right side out and draw a line 0.25-inches from the bottom. Starting at the seam on the back of the skirt, pin the black ribbon to the pencil line.

6 👥 Sew the ribbon on with black thread, using running stitch. This line of sewing will also keep the bottom hem in place.

7 Turn your material inside out again and run the elastic under the top hem of the skirt, with both ends poking out near the back seam.

8 Pin the hem in place. Draw a pencil line 1-inch from the top of the skirt and sew along the line. Make sure that the ends of the elastic are still poking out when you are finished!

9 When you have finished sewing the hem, take the two elastic ends and pull gently to gather the top of the skirt. Ask your child to put on the skirt and pull the elastic until the skirt fits her waist. Tie the ends together and snip off the spare elastic.

10 As a finishing touch, make a ribbon bow from wider black ribbon (see pages 16–17) and sew it to the front of the skirt.

All shopped out?
Why not stay home
and make your own?

Make your skirt summer-tastic! Cut out pretty daisies from felt and sew a row of them along the bottom. Add heart-shaped buttons. Finish with a pretty pink bow!

Minnie's fashion mood board

Feeling creative? Make yourself a funky collage inspired by Minnie's flawless fashion sense!

You will need:

- Templates on page 47
- Scissors
- Felt (pink, blue, and white)
- Craft glue and brush
- Double-sided tape
- Sequins
- Press-on bows
- Shiny cord
- Fabric (red and pink polka dot)
- Beads
- Buttons
- Tissue paper (red and pink polka dot)
- Posterboard (11.75in x 8.25in, blue)

If you don't have the exact things on the list, don't worry—a collage is a great way to use up leftover materials from other craft projects!

1 Using the templates on page 47, cut out a dress and two sleeves from pink felt. Ask your child to decorate the dress with sequins, a bow, and shiny cord. Make a second dress out of red polka-dot fabric and attach a bow at the waist.

2 Make a necklace by threading beads onto a cord and tying it in a bow. Use the template to make flowers from white felt, then glue buttons to their centers.

3 Using the template, cut out a handbag shape from blue felt. Help your child to decorate it with a bow, and glue on cord to form the handle. Next, cut the two-piece handbag from pink felt and polka-dot fabric, using the templates. Tape the fabric piece to the felt. Glue on cord for the handle and a button for the clasp.

4 👥 For the bow, trace the template onto the back of the pink polka-dot fabric. Cut the bow out of the fabric and cut a small strip of fabric for the middle piece. Wrap the strip around the middle of the bow and glue it in place.

5 👥 Cut out hearts from pink felt and ask your child to decorate them by gluing felt shapes, buttons, and sequins to their centers.

6 👥 To make a skirt, draw a small circle onto the tissue paper. Cut the circle out, then cut it in half. Fold the semicircle in half, then fold again, then fold once more. Cut a curve at the wide end of the cone shape. Open it out into a fan shape to make a skirt. Add a bow to the top.

Arrange all your items on the posterboard. Once you like the look, glue everything in place. Next step—admire your work!

Tip!
Use your Minnie stickers to add that special touch!

Stylish felt change purse

Make a change purse and keep your money safe—until you're ready to spend it on that perfect "must-have" accessory!

You will need:

- Templates on page 44
- Pencil (white)
- Scissors
- Felt (black, pale pink, dark pink, and white)
- Needle and thread (black, pink, and white)
- Pins
- Ribbon (red polka dot, 1in x 20in)
- Ribbon (red, 0.75in x 18in)
- Button

★ ★ ★

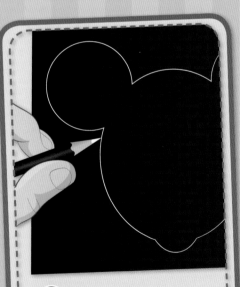

1 Using a white pencil, draw around the template of Minnie's head onto black felt. Cut out the shape.

2 Use the template to trace and cut out Minnie's face from pale pink felt. Using pink thread, sew it in position using running stitch (see page 4); only sew around the top half of Minnie's face.

3 Using the templates, trace and cut out the eyes, nose, and mouth pieces and sew them in place. Use thread that matches the color of the felt you are attaching.

4 Sew a line under Minnie's eyes. To make a solid line of stitching, sew one way in running stitch, then sew back along the same line to fill in the spaces.

5 Next, sew more black lines in the same way to make Minnie's long eyelashes and the details around her mouth.

6 For the back of the change purse, lay the face on black felt, pin in position, then cut to shape. Using pink thread, sew together around her chin. Change to black thread and sew around both sides of her upper face, leaving an opening at the top between her ears.

Tip!

If you don't have time to sew all the pieces of this project together, create your change purse using glue and fabric pens.

8 Tie the thinner ribbon around the middle of the bow and leave the ends loose. Sew the bow to the top layer of the change purse, between her ears.

9 Turn the change purse over and sew a button at the top of Minnie's head, between her ears. Tie the ribbon ends around the button to fasten the purse, then trim the ribbon ends if necessary.

7 Hold the polka-dot ribbon between your thumb and forefinger and fold it into four loops, two on each side of your thumb. Sew the loops down the middle, pull the thread tight, then tie a knot around the middle to make a bow.

There's no business like bow business!

Now that you know how to sew, you can make a Daisy Duck change purse, too. Use pink, blue, white, orange, and yellow felt and finish with a big bow made of bright pink ribbon.

33

Pretty as a picture frame!

Minnie keeps a picture of Clarabelle in her photo frame, because it reminds her of two of her favorite things—friendship and shoes!

You will need:

- Templates on page 47
- Card stock (8.5in x 11in, black and yellow)
- Pencil (white and No. 3)
- Scissors
- Double-sided tape
- Craft foam (yellow)
- Ruler
- Stickers from sticker sheet

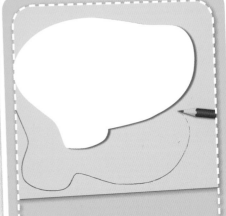

1 Trace the shoe template and larger oval template on page 47. Cut them out and draw around the shapes onto yellow card.

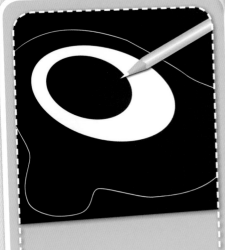

2 Next, ask your child to draw around the shoe template and smaller oval shape onto black card.

3 Cut both shapes out, as shown. Using double-sided tape, carefully stick the yellow card on top of the black card.

4 Trace two shoes, with larger ovals inside them, onto yellow craft foam. Using the template, trace two bows onto the foam. Cut out all the shapes.

5 Using double-sided tape carefully stick one of the foam shoes on top of the black card.

6 Use double-sided tape to stick the other foam shoe on top for double thickness.

7 To make the stand, cut out one strip of yellow card 5.5in x 1.5in. Use a pencil and ruler to make marks at 1.25in, 2.75in, and 4.25in. Make folds at the marks, then fold the strip up to make a triangle. Tape the triangle to make it secure, then stick it to the back of the frame.

Decorate your frame with your stickers and stick your favorite photo inside!

You can create picture frames for all your friends by using different colors of craft foam for each frame.

Minnie's sweet treats

Minnie's chic little cupcakes taste as good as they look—and they're super easy to make!

You will need:

For 12 cupcakes:
- Mixing bowl
- Hand whisk or electric mixer
- ½ cup butter, softened
- ½ cup granulated sugar
- 2 eggs, lightly beaten
- ⅔ cup self-raising flour
- ¼ cup cocoa powder
- Sieve and spoon
- 1 tablespoon milk
- Cupcake pan
- Baking cups
- Wire rack

For the icing and decoration:
- Ready-rolled icing (black and red)
- Rolling pin
- Parchment paper
- Knife
- Writing icing (white)
- 2⅓ cups confectioners' sugar
- ¾ butter, softened
- 1–2 tablespoons whole milk
- Piping bag with round nozzle
- Sugar balls and edible glitter

1 Pre-heat the oven to 350°F. Ask your child to beat the butter and sugar together until pale and fluffy. Add the eggs and beat until smooth.

2 Sift the flour and cocoa powder into the mixture and stir in gently. Mix in the milk and stir. Line a 12-hole cupcake tin with baking cups.

3 Help your child spoon the mixture into baking cups, until about half-full. Bake for 15 minutes, then place the cupcakes on a wire rack and let them cool completely.

4 To make Minnie ears, ask your child to roll out 2oz of black icing to 0.25-inches thick. Use the end of your piping nozzle to cut circles in the icing. Cut out 24 ears and put them on a sheet of parchment paper to set.

5 For the bows, ask your child to roll out 4oz of red icing to about 1.25-inches thick. Cut strips 4in x 0.75in, plus smaller pieces for the middle of the bows.

6 Fold the ends of a long strip into the center and press down firmly. Add a little dab of writing icing at the center and lay a small strip over it.

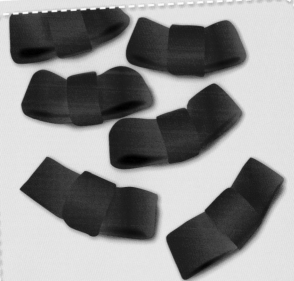

7 Wrap the small strip around the bow, turn it over, and add another dab of writing icing on the back. Press the ends of the strip down, turn it over, and leave until set. Make 11 more bows in the same way.

8 To make the buttercream frosting, add half the confectioners' sugar to the softened butter and ask your child to beat the mixture until it is smooth. Add the rest of the confectioners' sugar and a little milk and beat again until smooth and creamy. Add more milk, if necessary.

9 👥 Spoon the mixture into a piping bag with a nozzle. Pipe the buttercream onto each cake, working in a spiral, from the outside to the middle.

10 Allow the cupcakes to stand for about five minutes, then push two ears and a bow into each cake. Use sugar balls to add extra decoration, then add a final sprinkle of edible glitter.

Try out different designs for the tops of your cupcakes! Yummy!

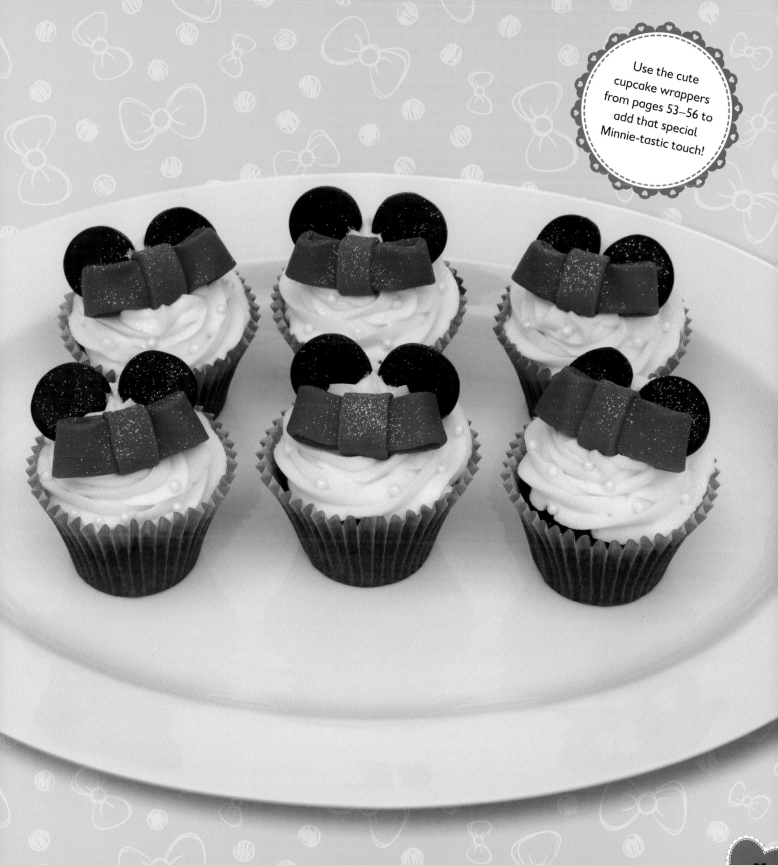

Use the cute cupcake wrappers from pages 53–56 to add that special Minnie-tastic touch!

39

I love handbags!

If you're a huge fan of handbags like Minnie,
this adorable door hanger is just made for you!

You will need:

- Jam jar lid
- Pencil
- Thick posterboard (red, 3in x 11in)
- Scissors
- Templates on page 46
- Ribbon (pink polka dot, 0.75in x 20in)
- Craft glue and brush
- Sequins
- Fabric (pink polka dot)

- Card stock (pink)
- Felt (blue, pink, and white)
- Stick-on bows
- Buttons
- Glitter glue (silver)
- Paintbrush
- Double-sided tape
- Ribbon (red polka dot, 0.75in x 20in)
- Black pen
- Stickers on sticker sheet

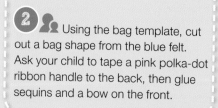

1 Using a jam jar lid, draw a semicircle at the top of the thick red posterboard, then cut it out. Cut little curved corners at the other end.

2 Using the bag template, cut out a bag shape from the blue felt. Ask your child to tape a pink polka-dot ribbon handle to the back, then glue sequins and a bow on the front.

3 For the second bag, use the rectangle template to cut the shape out of pink card. Then use the tabbed rectangle template to cut the shape out of pink polka-dot fabric. Glue the fabric to the top of the card to make the handbag flap. Cut a heart shape out of pink felt and glue on the bag. Add a button on the heart.

4 Use the flower template to cut flowers out of the white felt. Glue a button to the middle of each flower, then ask your child to brush glitter glue onto the petals.

5 Cut two 4-inch lengths from the pink polka-dot ribbon. Take the ends of each piece to the middle and tape in place. Tape the two pieces together. Wrap a short piece of the ribbon around the middle and tape it at the back. Cut the ribbon ends at an angle.

6 Tape the bags, flowers, and bow to the red posterboard. Fill in the spaces with your flower and heart stickers. To make your creation into a hanger, cut two equal lengths of red polka-dot ribbon and tape to the back of the posterboard at the top. Write your name on the hanger!

Anna's

Room

Be a fashion designer!

This sweet T-shirt is the perfect way to tell the world that your style icon is ... Minnie Mouse!

You will need:

- Pen
- 2 large sponges
- Bowl
- Scissors
- Old newspapers
- Plain T-shirt
- Fabric paint (black)
- Jam jar lid
- Iron

Tip!

You can cut shapes out of potatoes or pencil erasers and use them to make prints, too!

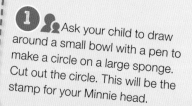

1 Ask your child to draw around a small bowl with a pen to make a circle on a large sponge. Cut out the circle. This will be the stamp for your Minnie head.

2 Cover your work surface with newspapers, then put a newspaper inside the T-shirt to stop the paint from seeping through to the back.

3 Put fabric paint into a bowl and dip your sponge in it so that paint covers the whole surface. Help your child press the sponge firmly onto the center of the T-shirt. Carefully lift off the sponge, leaving a black circle on the fabric.

4 Ask your child to draw around a jam jar lid on a sponge to make a smaller circular stamp for the ears. Dip the sponge in the paint and press down on the fabric to make two ears. Leave the T-shirt to dry.

Tip!
Iron the T-shirt to fix the fabric paint. Make sure to follow the manufacturer's instructions.

You could print lots of Minnie heads on one T-shirt. Why not decorate your creations by adding little bows? Or by sewing a frilly ribbon at the bottom of your T-shirt!

Templates

Pages 30–33 Minnie change purse

Pages 16–17 Headband ear

Pages 6-7 Party hats

Pages 18-19 Tote bag

Pages 8-9
Bow-tastic shoes

Pages 22-23 Bag charm

Feet

Face

Hand

Pages 20-21 Pencil pot

Pages 40-41 Door hanger

Sleeve

Bag 1

Bag 2 top

Dress

Pages 28-29
Fashion collage

Bag 2 bottom

Pages 34-35 Photo frame

Press-out makes

Create Minnie-tastic masterpieces with these fabulous press-out crafts! All you need to do is press out the pieces from pages 49–64 and follow the instructions.

Cute cupcake wrappers

Minnie's mini jewelry box

Minnie's clutch bag

Minnie's picnic basket

Minnie's picnic basket

1. Carefully press out all the shapes from pages 59–64 and fold along the pre-creased lines.
2. Fold up the handle and slot it into the sides of the bottom.
3. Form the bottom by matching the blue and purple tabs and slotting them together.
4. Attach the purple and blue tabs on the picnic basket lid to the ones on the bottom. Tuck in the flap on the underside of the lid.
5. Fold in all four sides of the bottom and flatten them to make a neat box shape.
6. Slot the plates and saucers inside the lid and put the other items inside the picnic basket. Close it by fitting the three tabs on the top of the lid to the slots in the bottom.

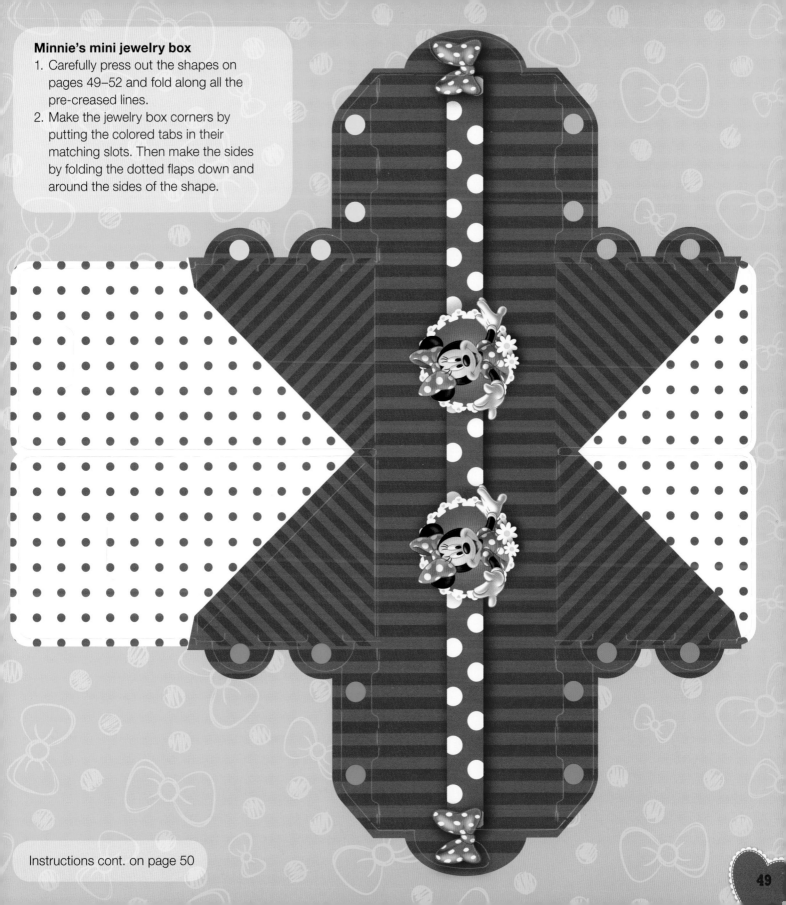

Minnie's mini jewelry box

1. Carefully press out the shapes on pages 49–52 and fold along all the pre-creased lines.

2. Make the jewelry box corners by putting the colored tabs in their matching slots. Then make the sides by folding the dotted flaps down and around the sides of the shape.

Instructions cont. on page 50

Minnie's mini jewelry box continued

3. Insert the base (page 51) along the bottom of the box.
4. Make a drawer (page 51) by slotting together the matching colored tabs, then folding down all four sides. Repeat for the second drawer.

© Disney

5. Push the tabs on the drawers into the slots on the bottom and the sides of the box.
6. Put your tiny treasures in the drawers, then close the box by slotting together the two halves of Minnie's bow.

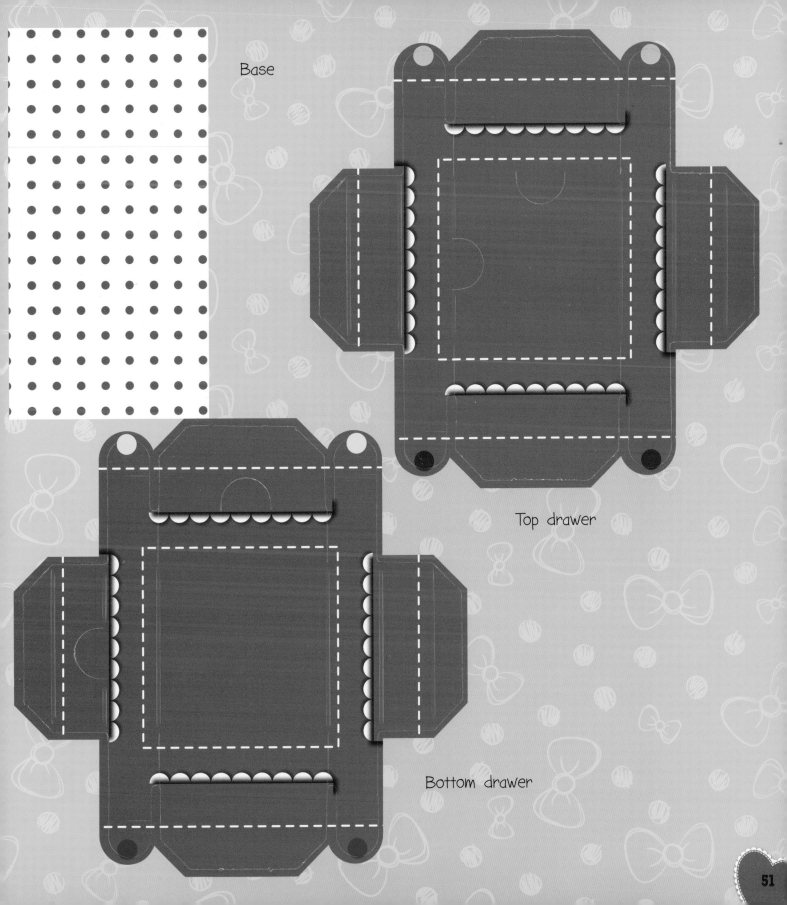

Base

Top drawer

Bottom drawer

51

© Disney

© Disney

© Disney

52

Cute cupcake wrappers

1. Carefully press out all of the shapes.
2. Push the tab at the end of the wrapper into the slot at the other end. Place a cupcake in the middle of each wrapper. Wow! You're ready for a fabulous Minnie tea party!

© Disney

© Disney

© Disney

© Disney

© Disney

© Disney

Minnie's clutch bag

1. Carefully press out the shape and fold along all the pre-creased lines. Using a glue stick, put glue down the length of the white tabs.
2. Fold into a bag shape and press the tabs to glue the bag together. Leave to dry.
3. Close the bag by slotting the tab under Minnie's bow.

© Disney

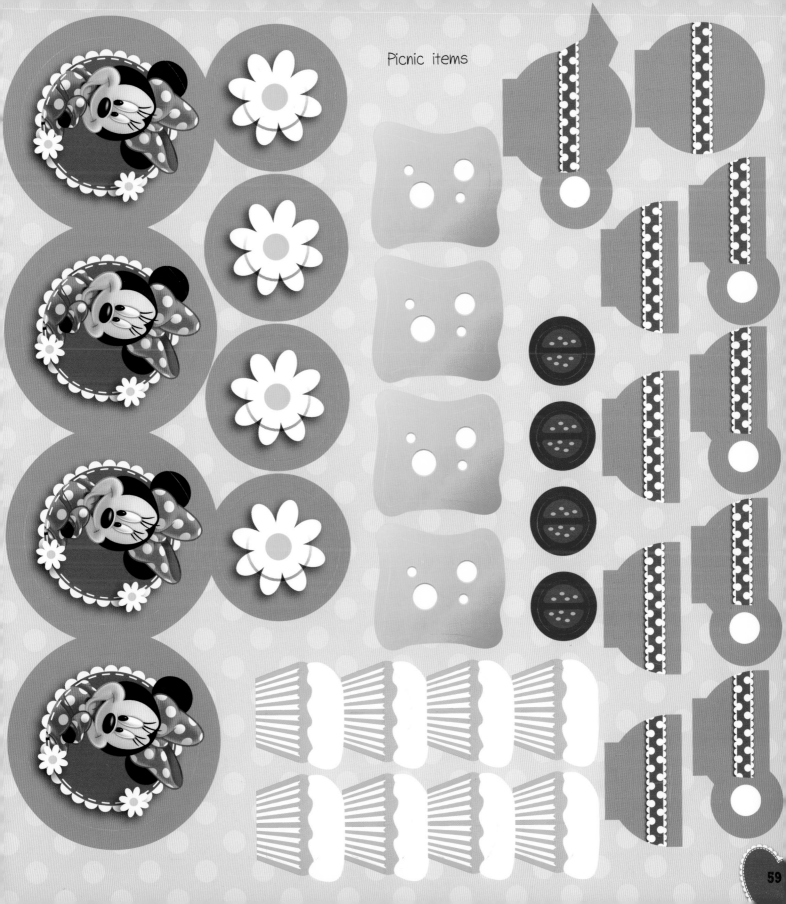

Picnic items

59

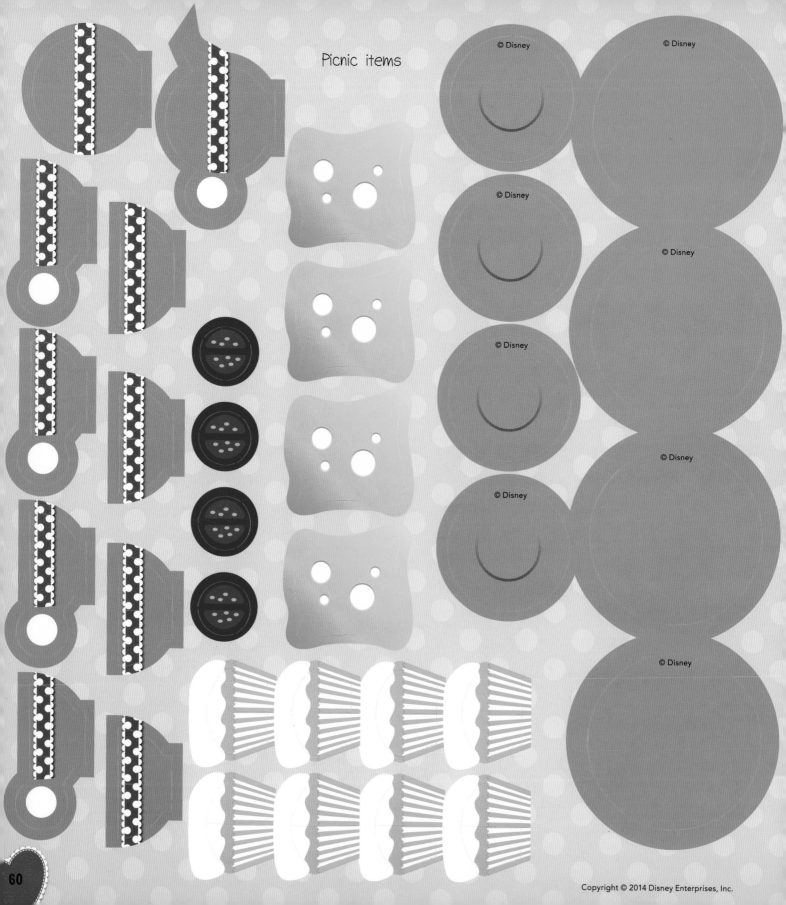

Picnic items

60

Basket base

61

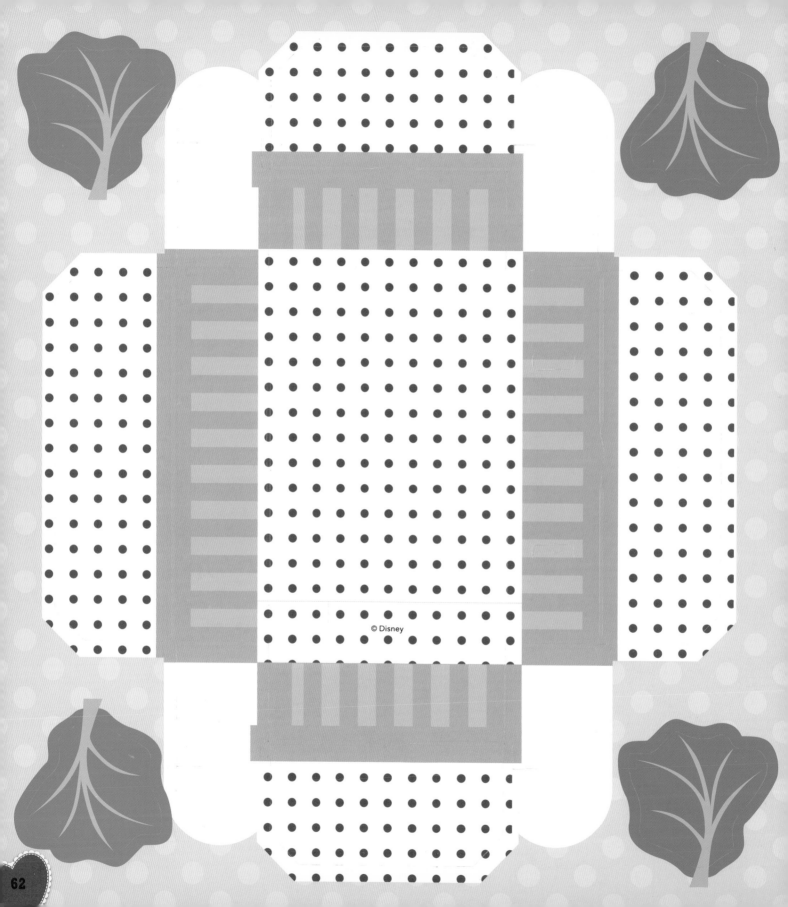

© Disney

Basket lid and handle

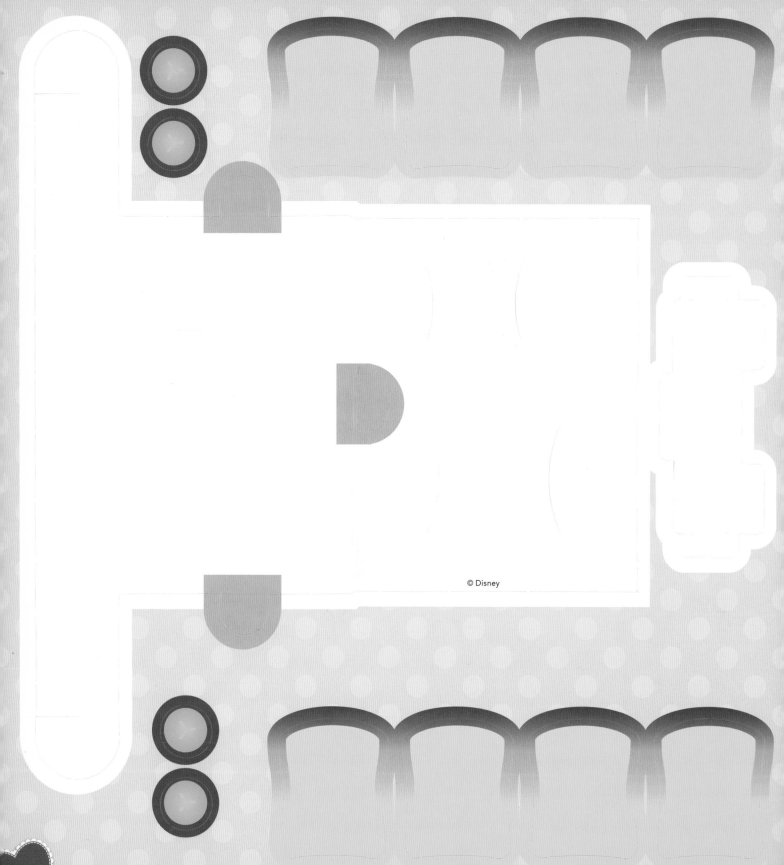

© Disney